1·05ᵖ

D0657030

ASTERIX AND GOLDEN SICKLE

TEXT BY GOSCINNY

DRAWINGS BY UDERZO

TRANSLATED BY ANTHEA BELL AND DEREK HOCKRIDGE

HODDER & STOUGHTON

LONDON LEICESTER SYDNEY AUCKLAND

ASTERIX IN OTHER LANGUAGES

Arab Countries	Dar el Maaref, 1119 Cornichel Nil, Cairo, Egypt
Australia	Hodder & Stoughton Children's Books, Salisbury Road, Leicester, LE1 7QS, England
Austria	Delta Verlag, Postfach 1215-7, Stuttgart 1, R.F.A.
Belgium	Dargaud Benelux, 3 rue Kindermans, 1050 Brussels
Brazil	Cedibra, rue Filomena Nunes 162, Rio de Janeiro
Brittany	(Breton) Armor Diffusion, 59 rue Duhamel, 35100 Rennes
Canada	Dargaud Canada Ltee, 300 Place d'Youville, Suite 31, Montreal, H2Y 2B6
Denmark	Gutenberghus Bladene, Vognmagergade 11, 1148 Copenhagen K
Finland	Sanoma Osakeyhtio, Ludviginkatu 2-10, 00130 Helsinki 12
German Federal Republic	Delta Verlag, Postfach 1215, 7 Stuttgart 1, R.F.A.
Holland	Dargaud Benelux, 3 rue Kindermans, 1050 Brussels
Hong Kong	Hodder & Stoughton Children's Books, Salisbury Road, Leicester, LE1 7QS, England
Iceland	Fjolvi Hf, Raudalak 20, Reykjavik
Italy	Arnoldo Mondadori Editore, Via Bianca de Savoia 20 20122, Milan
Latin America	Ediciones Junior S.A., 386 Aragon, Barcelona 9, Spain
New Zealand	Hodder & Stoughton Children's Books, Salisbury Road, Leicester, LE1 7QS, England
Norway	A/S Hjemmet (Gutenberghus Group) Kristian den 4des Gate 12, Oslo 1
Portugal	Livreria Bertrand, Aptdo 37, Rua Joao de Deus-Venda Nova, Amadora
Roman Empire	(Latin) Delta Verlag, Postfach 1215, 7 Stuttgart 1, R.F.A.
South Africa	(English) Hodder & Stoughton Children's Books, Salisbury Road, Leicester, LE1 7QS, England
	(Afrikaans) Human & Rousseau, Publishers (Pty) Ltd, State House, 3-9 Rose Street, Cape Town
Spain	(Castilian) Ediciones Junior S.A. 386 Aragon, Barcelona 9
	(Catalan, Basque, Galician) Ediciones Gaisa, Avenida Marques del Turia 67, Valencia
Sweden	Hemmets Journal Forlag (Gutenberghus Group) Fack 200 22 Malmo
Switzerland	Interpress S.A., En Budron B 1052, Le Mont/Lausanne
Turkey	Kervan Kitabcilik, Serefendi Sokagi 31, Cagaloglu-Istanbul
United Kingdom	Hodder & Stoughton Children's Books, Salisbury Road, Leicester LE1 7QS, England
Wales	(Welsh) Gwasg Y Dref Wen, 6 Rookwood Close, Llandaff, Cardiff
Yugoslavia	Nip Forum Vojvode Misica 1-3, 2100 Novi Sad

ISBN 0 340 20209 2 (cased edition)
ISBN 0 340 21209 8 (paperbound edition)

Copyright © 1962 Dargaud Editeur
English-language text copyright © 1975 Hodder & Stoughton Ltd

First published in Great Britain in 1975 (cased) by
Brockhampton Press Ltd (now Hodder & Stoughton Children's Books)

First published in Great Britain (paperbound) 1977

2 3 4 5 6 7 (cased edition)
1 2 3 4 5 6 (paperbound edition)

Printed in Great Britain for Hodder & Stoughton Children's Books,
a division of Hodder & Stoughton Ltd, Arlen House,
Salisbury Road, Leicester by Morrison & Gibb Ltd, Edinburgh

All rights reserved. No part of this publication may be
reproduced or transmitted in any form or by any means,
electronic or mechanical, including photocopy, recording,
or any information storage and retrieval system, without
permission in writing from the publisher

The year is 50 BC. Gaul is entirely occupied by the Romans. Well, not entirely... One small village of indomitable Gauls still holds out against the invaders. And life is not easy for the Roman legionaries who garrison the fortified camps of Totorum, Aquarium, Laudanum and Compendium...

a few of the Gauls

Asterix, the hero of these adventures. A shrewd, cunning little warrior; all perilous missions are immediately entrusted to him. Asterix gets his superhuman strength from the magic potion brewed by the druid Getafix...

Obelix, Asterix's inseparable friend. A menhir delivery-man by trade; addicted to wild boar. Obelix is always ready to drop everything and go off on a new adventure with Asterix — so long as there's wild boar to eat, and plenty of fighting.

Getafix, the venerable village druid. Gathers mistletoe and brews magic potions. His speciality is the potion which gives the drinker superhuman strength. But Getafix also has other recipes up his sleeve...

Cacofonix, the bard. Opinion is divided as to his musical gifts. Cacofonix thinks he's a genius. Everyone else thinks he's unspeakable. But so long as he doesn't speak, let alone sing, everybody likes him...

Finally, Vitalstatistix, the chief of the tribe. Majestic, brave and hot-tempered, the old warrior is respected by his men and feared by his enemies. Vitalstatistix himself has only one fear; he is afraid the sky may fall on his head tomorrow. But as he always says, 'Tomorrow never comes.'

Asterix and the Golden Sickle

THE FIERCELY INDEPENDENT LITTLE VILLAGE WHERE ASTERIX AND THE OTHER GAULS LIVE IS AT PEACE....

GOOD HUNTING, ASTERIX?

NOTHING MUCH TODAY...

OBELIX IS HAPPILY AT WORK, CARVING OUT A MENHIR...

THERE'LL ALWAYS BE A GAU-AAUL!

CACOFONIX THE BARD IS GIVING THE CHILDREN LESSONS...

WELL, YOUNG MAN, AND INTO HOW MANY PARTS IS GAUL DIVIDED?

$VIII \times V = XL$

$\begin{array}{r} III \\ + I \\ \hline = IV \end{array}$

?

IN SHORT, EVERYONE IS CONTENTED. ALL IS PEACE AND PLENTY...

ANOTHER BOAR, OBELIX?

YES, PLEASE!

WHEN SUDDENLY...

OH, BY TOUTATIS!

??? ? ?

WHAT'S ALL THAT SHOUTING?

IT'S THE VOICE OF OUR DRUID GETAFIX!

IT'S COMING FROM THAT OAK TREE OVER THERE!

SCRGNGNGNONRR... ARCHRGHGHN... GNEUGNEU...

WHAT'S THE MATTER, O DRUID?

BY BELENOS, TOUTATIS AND BELISAMA! I'VE BROKEN MY GOLDEN SICKLE!

!

THIS IS TERRIBLE! MISTLETOE MUST BE CUT WITH A GOLDEN SICKLE IF IT IS TO HAVE MAGIC POWERS!

IT COULDN'T BE WORSE TIMED! I HAVE TO START SOON FOR THE FOREST OF THE CARNUTES TO ATTEND THE GREAT ANNUAL CONFERENCE OF GAULISH DRUIDS. I CAN'T GO WITHOUT A SICKLE!

ALL YOU HAVE TO DO IS BUY ANOTHER ONE!

GOOD SICKLES DON'T GROW ON TREES!

THE BEST, INDEED THE ONLY ONES I CONSIDER WORTH USING, ARE MADE BY THE FAMOUS METALLURGIX, IN FARAWAY LUTETIA...

HE'S RIGHT. IT'S WELL KNOWN THAT METALLURGIX MAKES THE BEST SICKLES...

YOU'RE RIGHT THERE...

AND LUTETIA IS A LONG WAY OFF... YOU HAVE TO PASS THROUGH FORESTS FULL OF BARBARIANS AND BANDITS TO GET THERE!

I AM PREPARED TO GO TO LUTETIA, O DRUID!

NEXT MORNING!!!

Auf wiedersehen!

The Com Barbar

HEY, ASTERIX, WHY DO YOU THINK THAT TRAVELLER TOLD US SICKLES WERE IN SHORT SUPPLY IN LUTETIA?

NO IDEA, OBELIX.

LET'S ENJOY OUR JOURNEY; WE CAN WORRY ABOUT THAT LATER...

THE ROMANS ARE RUINING THE LANDSCAPE WITH ALL THESE MODERN BUILDINGS!

OUR FRIENDS' JOURNEY PROCEEDS WITHOUT MUCH INCIDENT, APART FROM A FEW SCUFFLES WITH BANDITS...

AT SUINDINUM, ASTERIX AND OBELIX ARE UNABLE TO FIND A BED, AS IT HAPPENS TO BE THE DAY OF THE GREAT OX-CART RACE, THE SUINDINUM 24 HOURS...

BUT AT LAST, ONE DAY...

LOOK! OBELIX!

LUTETIA!

ISN'T IT BIG!

13

14

17

AND ALL RAIDS LEAD TO ROME AND THE CIRCUS MAXIMUS! LET'S GET OUT OF HERE!

?

WHAT'S UP? IS IT OVER ALREADY?

BY JUPITER! ANYONE MIGHT THINK WE WERE IN POMPEII!

OAKS

SHALL WE CARRY ON?

NO, IT WOULD BE BETTER TO EXPLAIN!

DID YOU DO ALL THIS?

YES, AND WE WERE VERY RESTRAINED!

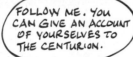

FOLLOW ME. YOU CAN GIVE AN ACCOUNT OF YOURSELVES TO THE CENTURION.

VADE RETRO! MOVE ALONG THERE! VADE RETRO!

19

BOOHOO! POOR COUSIN METALLURGIX!

WE'LL FIND HIM, OBELIX. FOR A START, WHAT DOES YOUR COUSIN LOOK LIKE?

WHAT DOES HE LOOK LIKE? I'VE NO IDEA. I'VE NEVER SET EYES ON HIM.

!

LET'S GO BACK TO HIS HOUSE. WE MIGHT FIND A CLUE THERE...

SO WE MIGHT. HOW CAN I BE EXPECTED TO KNOW WHAT HE LOOKS LIKE WHEN I'VE NEVER SEEN HIM...? SOMETIMES ASTERIX JUST DOESN'T STOP TO THINK!

THE DOOR'S LOCKED, OF COURSE...

LEAVE IT TO ME, I'LL OPEN IT...

CRAAASH!

THERE YOU ARE!

WHAT A MESS! THAT'S FUNNY; WE'RE RATHER TIDY IN MY FAMILY...

THERE'S BEEN A FIGHT HERE. LOOK, METALLURGIX HAS LEFT HIS PERSONAL BELONGINGS AND HIS KITCHEN UTENSILS BEHIND...

BUT HIS TOOLS, HIS SICKLES AND HIS MONEY ARE ALL MISSING. OBELIX, YOUR COUSIN'S BEEN KIDNAPPED BY THE SICKLE-TRAFFICKERS!

BOOHOOOO! POOR METALLURGIX!

WELL, THIS PROVES METALLURGIX IS STILL ALIVE. WE'LL FIND HIM, BY TOUTATIS!

OH GOODY!

LET'S MOVE IN HERE, AND FIRST, LET'S GO AND DO SOME SHOPPING.

GOOD IDEA!

LATER...

WHAT A PRICE BOAR IS IN LUTETIA!

AND THE BUTCHER SAID PRICES WERE GOING TO RISE EVEN HIGHER. IT'S A POOR LOOKOUT FOR GAUL!

THE SUN, RISING ON LUTETIA, IS GREETED BY A COCKEREL...

COCK-A-DOODLE-DO!

GET UP, OBELIX! IT'S TIME TO START OUR INVESTIGATIONS!

THAT'S RIGHT. WE MUST FIND METALLURGIX.

LET'S GO BACK TO THAT ARVERNIAN IN THE WINE SHOP. I'M SURE HE KNOWS SOMETHING!

THE SUN OF MASSILIA

OH!

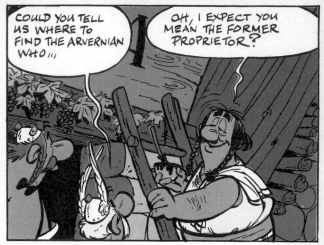

COULD YOU TELL US WHERE TO FIND THE ARVERNIAN WHO...

OH, I EXPECT YOU MEAN THE FORMER PROPRIETOR?

THAT CRAZY GAUL WHO SOLD ME THIS PLACE FOR A HANDFUL OF BRONZE COINS! IT'S UNDER NEW MANAGEMENT NOW, BUT YOU WON'T BE DISAPPOINTED!

I CAN OFFER YOU MY SPECIALITY: FISH SOUP! MADE OF NICE FRESH FISH, JUST ARRIVED BY OX-CART FROM MASSILIA!

DO YOU KNOW WHERE THE ARVERNIAN HAS GONE?

OH! HE STARTED FOR GERGOVIA THIS MORNING, TRAVELLING BY OX-CART, THE SAME AS THE FISH!

THE SUN OF MASSILIA

WHAT A SHAME! IF YOU'D COME A LITTLE SOONER YOU'D HAVE FOUND HIM STILL HERE!

THANKS!

ALL THESE LUTETIANS ARE CRAZY, BY BELISAMA!

WE'LL CATCH UP WITH THE ARVERNIAN ON THE WAY TO GERGOVIA.

RIGHT!

HE CAN'T HAVE GOT FAR, AND ON FOOT WE'RE AS FAST AS ANY OX-CART!

OF COURSE WE ARE! THE OXEN ARE ON FOOT TOO!

CAN YOU TELL ME THE WAY TO GERGOVIA, PLEASE?

TAKE ROMAN ROAD VII.

WHAT A LOT OF TRAFFIC!

THERE MUST OFTEN BE AMPHORA-NECKS ON FINE DAYS!

SLOW! SLAVES AT WORK

THAT'S WHAT I CALL REAL DRIVING!

THEY'RE CRAZY! JUST KEEP AN EYE ON YOUR OXEN! ACCIDENTS CAN HAPPEN SO QUICKLY!

I STILL DON'T SEE OUR ARVERNIAN FRIEND...

MAYBE THAT CART AT THE TOP OF THE HILL THERE...

IT'S.... IT'S THEM!

THE ARVERNIAN! IN FRONT THERE!

LET'S GO!

AND THE GREAT RACE IS ON!

GEE UP! GEE UP!

I'M GOING TO OVERTAKE!

BONG!

WHAT'S THE MATTER? WHAT DO YOU WANT?

WHERE'S METALLURGIX? TELL US ALL YOU KNOW!

NOT TALKING, EH?

STOP! STOP!

LEAVE HIM TO ME, ASTERIX! LET ME HAVE A GO!

ONE DAY SOME MEN CAME AND TOOK METALLURGIX AWAY... I HAPPENED TO BE PASSING, AND THEY WERE GOING TO TAKE ME TOO...

BUT ONE OF THE MEN, CALLED CLOVOGARLIX, LET ME GO ON CONDITION I TOLD HIM IF ANYONE CAME LOOKING FOR METALLURGIX. THEY FORCED ME TO BE THEIR ACCOMPLICE, BUT I'M INNOCENT REALLY!

RIGHT! THE ARVERNIAN HAS GIVEN US CLOVOGARLIX'S ADDRESS... WE'LL GO THERE!

WE OUGHT TO HAVE KEPT ONE OF THE OXEN FOR A SNACK...

I'LL NEVER SET FOOT IN LUTETIA AGAIN!

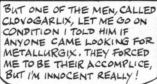

20

WARM RAYS OF BRILLIANT SUNSHINE LIGHT UP A CLOUDLESS SKY....

... LITTLE BIRDS WARBLE ON THE LEAFY BRANCHES ...

... SQUIRRELS PLAY ON THE MOSSY GROUND ...

... WHILE UNDERNEATH THE MOSSY GROUND....

BO NG PLAF! OUCH!

GET THEM OBELIX!

YOU BET I WILL, ASTERIX!

BOUM!

ARE THERE ANY LEFT, ASTERIX?

NO, OBELIX, YOU'RE JUST FINISHING OFF THE LAST ONE ....

BONG! BONG! BONG!

LET'S GET OUT OF HERE AND WARN THE BOSS!

OBELIX, I'M A BIT WORRIED.... I CAN'T FIND NAVISHTRIX!

HE CAN'T HAVE COME TO ANY HARM. HE WAS HERE JUST NOW!

ANYWAY, I'VE GOT CLOVOGARLIX.

THAT'S SOMETHING....

35

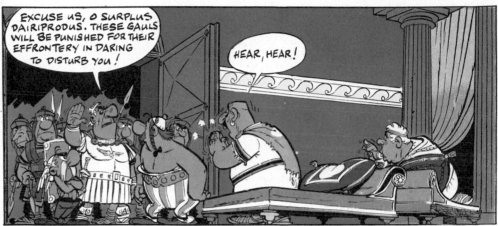